# A Sticky
# Situation

**Written by**  **Illustrated by**
**Catherine Coe** **Jan McCafferty**

ORCHARD

/e J
For Louise
C.C.

For Rose and Max, I hope you have
lots of fun adventures together! xx
J.McC.

Reading Consultant: Prue Goodwin, Lecturer in literacy and children's books

ORCHARD BOOKS
338 Euston Road, London NW1 3BH
*Orchard Books Australia*
Hachette Children's Books
Level 17/207 Kent Street, Sydney NSW 2000

First published in 2011 by Orchard Books
First paperback publication in 2012

Text © Catherine Coe 2011
Illustrations © Jan McCafferty 2011

ISBN 978 1 40830 687 1 (hardback)
ISBN 978 1 40830 695 6 (paperback)

The rights of Catherine Coe to be identified as the author and
Jan McCafferty to be identified as the illustrator of this work
have been asserted by them in accordance with the
Copyright, Designs and Patents Act, 1988.

A CIP catalogue record for this book is available from the British Library.
All rights reserved.

1 3 5 7 9 10 8 6 4 2 (hardback)
1 3 5 7 9 10 8 6 4 2 (paperback)

Printed in China

Orchard Books is a division of Hachette Children's Books,
an Hachette UK company.

www.hachette.co.uk

It was Casper the Kid Cowboy's birthday. He was looking forward to his party – and to his birthday presents!

Casper's best friend, Pete,
arrived at the party first.
He gave Casper a new pair
of cowboy boots.

"Thank you, partner!"
Casper said.

Casper also got a brand-new shirt, a cowboy hat and some bright-red cowboy trousers.

But Casper's best present was saved until last. This present wouldn't stay still – and it was *very* big!

Then the present started to make funny noises . . .

Casper pulled away the sheet –
and underneath were two cows!

"Yee-ha!" Casper and Pete
shouted together.

Casper had dreamed of this day.

Now that he had his own cattle,

he could be a *real* cowboy!

The next morning, the two best friends woke at dawn. They couldn't wait to have a real cowboy adventure with Casper's new cows.

"I'm going to call this one Dora, and that one Daisy," Casper decided. But Dora and Daisy didn't seem interested in having adventures at all!

Finally, the two best friends set off with Dora and Daisy, herding them across the desert plains.

"This is mighty fine!" Casper called to Pete.

But Pete wasn't so happy.
Daisy had just tipped over the
water Pete had been carrying.
It had soaked Pete's horse,
Funny Fool.

Soon they were on the move again. Funny Fool dried off as they rode along.

"Yee-ha!" Pete shouted.

"We're *proper* cowboys now!" Casper said, smiling at his beloved horse, Blue the Brave.

But as the midday sun shone down, the cows started to look unwell.

"They're thirsty!" Casper realised. But there was no water left to give them.

"Oh no," Casper said. "Being a *real* cowboy isn't as easy as it looks."

"It's OK," Pete replied. "I can see some other cowboys up ahead. I'll ask them for water."

Pete galloped away on
Funny Fool, while Casper
stayed with Dora and Daisy.

Pete was gone for a long time. Casper was feeling thirsty now, too. And the cows were getting desperate!

"Sorry I took so long!" Pete shouted as he raced back. "It's Burt and Bruno! They say they'll give us water, but they want Dora in exchange."

Burt and Bruno were Casper's worst enemies. They were very mean and nasty.

"No way!" Casper replied. "Dora was my birthday present!"

Casper turned to the cows. They looked *really* thirsty. He knew he had to do something.

Blue the Brave and Funny
Fool needed water, too. So did
Casper and Pete! The sun was
beating down, and they were a
long ride from home.

Suddenly Casper remembered
his other birthday presents.
He had a plan!
"Wait here!" Casper told Pete,
as he rode off bravely to face
his enemies.

"Well, if it isn't Burt and Bruno!" Casper said, trying to look big and tough. "How do you like my new cowboy outfit?"

Burt and Bruno looked impressed. Their own clothes were old and dirty.

"I'll give you my new hat, shirt, trousers and boots – in exchange for some water," Casper said.

"Deal!" Bruno said quickly.

None of the new clothes fitted Burt and Bruno, but they didn't seem to mind!

Pete was surprised when Casper arrived back in his underwear! But he was *very* pleased to see the water.

"What happened?" Pete asked.
"I did a deal," Casper said.
"It was worth giving up my
other birthday presents, if it
meant I could keep Dora."

Dora, Daisy, Blue, Funny Fool, Casper and Pete all took turns to drink the water.

As the sun set, the two best friends rode home with Casper's cows. They really were *proper* cowboys – even if Casper didn't *look* like one without his clothes!

**Written by**  **Illustrated by**
**Catherine Coe** **Jan McCafferty**

All priced at £8.99

Orchard Books are available from all good bookshops,
or can be ordered from our website: www.orchardbooks.co.uk,
or telephone 01235 827702, or fax 01235 827703.

Prices and availability are subject to change.